To all the real-live Pennys
—J.W.

For Sarah
—B.S.

To share your Christmas Jar miracle, visit www.christmasjars.com

Text © 2009 Jason Wright
Illustrations © 2009 Ben Sowards

Visit us at ShadowMountain.com

Library of Congress Cataloging-in-Publication Data

Wright, Jason F.
  Penny's Christmas Jar miracle / Jason F. Wright ; illustrated by Ben Sowards.
      p. cm.
  Summary: Penny Paisley holds a party to present the family "Christmas Jar"—a jar in which her family has been saving spare change throughout the year—to an ailing neighbor, Grandpa Charlie.
  ISBN 978-1-60641-167-4 (hardbound : alk. paper)
  [1. Neighborliness—Fiction. 2. Christmas—Fiction. 3. Generosity—Fiction. 4. Parties—Fiction. 5. Coin banks—Fiction.]
  I. Sowards, Ben, ill. II. Title.
  PZ.W9492Pen 2009
  [E]—dc22
                                                          2009017677

Printed in the United States of America
Phoenix Color Corporation, Hagerstown, MD

10   9   8   7   6   5   4   3   2

Penny's Christmas Jar *Miracle*

Jason F. Wright
ILLUSTRATED BY BEN SOWARDS

SHADOW
MOUNTAIN

Penny Paisley loved Christmas. She loved the snow, the gifts, the decorations, and of course, setting up Penny's Hot Chocolate Stand. But most of all she loved the Christmas Jar, the Paisley family's most treasured tradition.

Throughout the year, each member of the family dropped their extra pennies, nickels, dimes, and quarters into a giant glass jar that Mrs. Paisley kept on the kitchen counter. With everyone so excited to collect change, it never took long for it to fill to the brim.

Then each December, Penny and her family made their most important decision of the entire year.

Who would receive the Paisley Family Christmas Jar?

She was sure this year would be the most special Christmas Jar ever, because it was her turn to choose who would receive the special gift, and she had a very fun idea to share.

When the night arrived to tell her family her idea, butterflies fluttered in Penny's stomach. She recalled the magical year they gave their Christmas Jar to a homeless man by the abandoned train station. Another year they had left it on the front doorstep of her brother Jeremy's teacher.

"I would like to do something different this year," Penny said. "What if instead of just giving our jar to only *one* person or *one* family, what if we gave it to the *entire neighborhood?* We could use the Christmas Jar money to have the biggest and best party anyone has ever, ever, ever been to. No one will *ever* forget it!"

Just as she hoped, everyone cheered her best idea ever.

The next day, Penny rushed home after school, as she did on most afternoons during the winter, and hurried to open Penny's Hot Chocolate Stand on the sidewalk in front of her house. That day, she had a lot of customers, but as always her two favorites were Grandpa Charlie and his dog, Pilgrim. Everyone knew Charlie wasn't really Penny's grandpa, but he looked like a grandpa and acted like a grandpa. And since he didn't have any grandchildren of his own, most of the people in Penny's neighborhood called him Grandpa Charlie, too.

"Hi, Lucky Penny," Grandpa Charlie said. She had lots of nicknames, but "Lucky Penny" was her favorite. "Would you do me a favor and take Pilgrim on his walk again tonight? He loves it when you take him."

"Of course," Penny answered. "Want to come with us?"

N ot this time, Lucky Penny. I'm a little tired today. But I'd still like that cup of hot chocolate." Grandpa Charlie smiled and handed her a dollar bill. "Keep the change." Grandpa Charlie winked because he knew her secret—all the money went into the Paisley Family Christmas Jar.

Penny motioned for Grandpa Charlie to lean down. "We're not giving away our jar this year," she whispered. "We're having a fancy party instead. I'm making invitations for everyone in the neighborhood. But *shhh*—it's still a secret."

Grandpa Charlie pretended to zip his lips shut. "That sounds like a wonderful idea. If you need help, you can knock on my door anytime." Grandpa Charlie winked again and walked home.

One extra-snowy day, Penny was packing up her hot chocolate stand when she realized that all of her regular customers had come for hot chocolate except for Grandpa Charlie. She took her things inside and quickly dumped her change in the Christmas Jar. Then Penny crossed the street to deliver a cup of hot chocolate to Grandpa Charlie and noticed that there was a sign on his red truck. It said FOR SALE.

Penny rang the doorbell. But it wasn't Grandpa Charlie who opened the door.

Instead, a woman in a bright blue shirt and nametag answered.

"Is Grandpa Charlie home?" Penny asked shyly.

Before the woman could answer, Penny heard Grandpa Charlie's voice from the other room. "Come in, Penny. I'm here."

Penny walked into the living room. "Oh!" she blurted. "Are you alright?"

"I'm a little under the weather, but I'll be fine."

"Is your truck sick, too?"

Grandpa Charlie laughed and coughed, almost at the same time. "No, dear, the old truck is just for sale. Sometimes it takes money *and* medicine to get better. I have lots of medicine, but not as much money."

"Will you be better soon?" Penny asked.

"I hope so. I sure don't want to miss your party." Pilgrim barked three times. "And it looks like Pilgrim doesn't want to miss his walk tonight. Would you like to take him for me again?"

"Sure," Penny said, and she gave him a gentle good-bye hug. Even though he didn't feel well, Grandpa Charlie smiled anyway.

As Penny left with Pilgrim, she noticed that Grandpa Charlie still hadn't put up a Christmas tree. Now she knew why.

Penny and Pilgrim walked slower than usual around their quiet neighborhood streets. Penny couldn't stop thinking about Grandpa Charlie and the tube in his arm. She would do anything to make him better . . . inside and out. As snow fell and tickled her cheeks, an idea began to grow. By the time she returned to Grandpa Charlie's, she had an idea as big as Christmas.

After dinner Penny shared her new idea with her family. They loved the idea so much. They said it was even better than her last idea.

"That's wonderful, Penny! We're very proud of you." Dad's eyes twinkled with excitement.

Penny had never felt so big.

The next day Penny couldn't wait to deliver Grandpa
Charlie's hot chocolate and take Pilgrim on his walk.
But it wasn't an ordinary walk. This time Penny carried
Pilgrim's leash in one hand and a basket with the Paisley Family
Christmas Jar in the other. They stopped at each neighbor's
home and Penny shared her secret. Everyone loved it, everyone
smiled, and Penny felt so warm inside she didn't think she even
needed a coat.

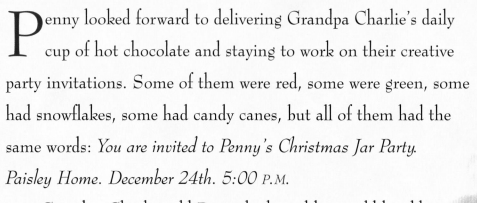

Penny looked forward to delivering Grandpa Charlie's daily cup of hot chocolate and staying to work on their creative party invitations. Some of them were red, some were green, some had snowflakes, some had candy canes, but all of them had the same words: *You are invited to Penny's Christmas Jar Party. Paisley Home. December 24th. 5:00 P.M.*

Grandpa Charlie told Penny he hoped he would be able to come, but even Penny could see that he still wasn't feeling well.

Penny was so excited when the day finally arrived to deliver the official invitations that she even let her brother, Jeremy, tag along. One by one they delivered the invitations to every house in the neighborhood. Everyone was excited, everyone promised to come, and Penny couldn't stop smiling all the way home.

Christmas Eve! At last! Penny was exhausted from working all day with her family making treats and decorations.

Right on schedule, the guests began arriving at five o'clock. She smiled when she noticed most of her neighbors were carrying something tucked inside colorful bags or baskets or wrapped tightly in scarves.

Penny welcomed them. "Come in, but don't take your coats off! It's *not* Christmas Eve yet!"

She was right. It didn't look *anything* like Christmas Eve in the Paisley home.

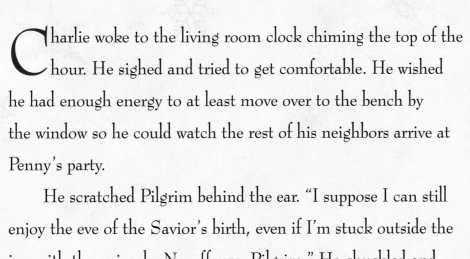

Charlie woke to the living room clock chiming the top of the hour. He sighed and tried to get comfortable. He wished he had enough energy to at least move over to the bench by the window so he could watch the rest of his neighbors arrive at Penny's party.

He scratched Pilgrim behind the ear. "I suppose I can still enjoy the eve of the Savior's birth, even if I'm stuck outside the inn with the animals. No offense, Pilgrim." He chuckled and hummed a few bars of his favorite Christmas carol as his eyelids grew heavy.

Then all at once the music wasn't just in his head anymore. He propped himself up to listen. Had he dozed off?

"Do you hear something, Pilgrim?"

But Pilgrim was already racing for the front door.

The Christmas tree came through the door first, carried carefully by Mr. Paisley with Penny following closely behind. She led what seemed like the entire neighborhood in singing "Joy to the World."

"*Now* it's Christmas Eve," Penny said as the singing ended and friends filled every corner of Grandpa Charlie's living room with homemade Christmas treats and their beautiful handmade decorations. Penny's dad set up the Christmas tree by the fireplace.

Grandpa Charlie was astonished. "What is all this, Penny?"

"It's Grandpa Charlie's Christmas Jars party!"

Penny handed him the Paisley Family Christmas Jar and kissed him on the cheek.
"Merry Christmas, Grandpa Charlie."

Many of the other guests also had a surprise for him. One at a time they shook his hand or gave him a kind hug and presented their own Christmas Jar. Some were big, some were small, some were decorated, and some were plain, but every jar was full.

As everyone enjoyed the Christmas Jars party, Grandpa Charlie leaned in close and in a hoarse whisper asked, "Lucky Penny, are all these jars full of money really for me?"

Y es, Grandpa Charlie, but they're not full of money.
They're full of *love*."

Though her vision blurred with tears as she looked into
Grandpa Charlie's watery eyes, she saw something as clearly as the
bright star that had once shone in the night sky over Bethlehem.

"This wasn't a party after all," Penny said. "It was a miracle."

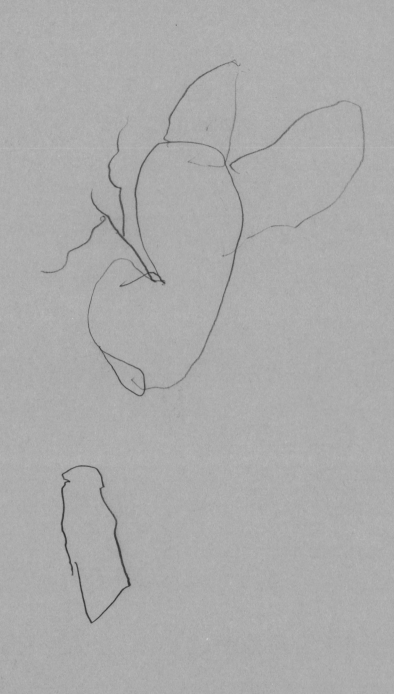